SMASHER

MARGOT SUNDERLAND

Illustrated by Nicky Armstrong

HINTONHOUSE

Simon Asher, known as Smasher, was good at being bad.

He bullied little kids, broke into cars, locked his brother in cupboards and got drunk. He kicked doors, threw furniture and smashed windows.

Just for the buzz of it.

Smasher never felt guilty. 'What does it matter in this lousy world?' he thought.

But for some reason, all the smashing didn't make Smasher happy.

Powerful yes. Happy no.

SMASHER

Published by
Hinton House Publishers Ltd
Newman House, 4 High Street, Buckingham MK18 1NT, UK
info@hintonpublishers.com
www.hintonpublishers.com

Printed in the United Kingdom by Hobbs the Printers Ltd

British Library Cataloguing in Publication Data
A catalogue record for this book is available from the British Library

ISBN 978-1-906531-10-2

FSC
Mixed Sources
Product group from well-managed
forests and other controlled sources
Cert no. SA-COC-001530
www.fsc.org
© 1996 Forest Stewardship Council

For years, Smasher had hated being a kid. He'd spent all his time just waiting to grow up, waiting to be big enough to get his revenge for every bad thing that had ever happened to him.

He remembered all the times he'd been bullied, shouted at, called names and hit.

He'd waited so many years, and now aged fourteen-and-a-half, he felt he'd arrived.

For Smasher, it was pay back time.

One day, when Smasher was waiting outside the Head's office for flooding the boy's toilets and setting off the school's fire alarm, some builders walked past. They'd come to build a climbing wall in the gym.

Smasher felt a rush of excitement at the very thought. He'd been on a climbing wall once before on a summer holiday. It was cool.

Smasher had learned fast.

IN TROUBLE AT SCHOOL ... AGAIN!
HEADMASTER'S OFFICE
Cool! A new climbing wall in the gym. I can do that!

The climbing wall was soon ready in the gym.

Smasher loved it. He felt as if he was climbing up the side of the whole world, climbing up, up to the sky, to the clouds, above the whole wide world.

One afternoon, during a really good lesson on the climbing wall, with all sorts of cool new moves, Grant, the climbing instructor, pointed to Smasher.

'OK everyone, let's watch Simon Asher. See how he thinks before he makes his next move. See how he gets his weight really balanced, so that each step up the wall looks easy.'

After the session, Grant asked Smasher to wait behind. 'Look kid you've got real talent,' he said. 'Can you join the climbing club? We go rock climbing in the country once a month.'

At that moment, Smasher felt different about EVERYTHING. Grant was seeing him like no one had ever seen him before.

All his life, people had been saying, 'There goes Smasher messing up again.'

And now here was Grant saying, 'Here comes Smasher being really cool.'

It was like Grant was holding up a huge great mirror, not with the usual cracks and broken bits, but a bright shiny mirror, making Smasher see himself like never before.

But soon his old feelings – that he was scum – came flooding back.

'Look man, if you really knew about me', he began.

'I do know about you', said Grant, 'And all the crazy things you've done in this school, but I'm talking to Simon Asher the cool climber, not Simon the Smasher!'

On the way back to the classroom, Smasher felt on top of the world. He now had two things he loved, smashing *and* climbing. He felt a kind of glow that he'd never felt before.

Then this big kid, Smithie came hurtling down the corridor in a big hurry. He accidentally knocked Smasher.

Smasher's blood started to boil. He went for Smithie, tearing into his shirt, pushing him to the ground. Smithie screamed with fear and pain, but Smasher carried on laying into him. Smithie had a huge gash over one eye and a bloody nose.

At times like this, Smasher even shocked *himself*. All that rage, as if from nowhere.

Mr Todd, the history teacher, marched Smasher to the Headteacher's office. 'But sir he was dissing me, he was dissing me!' screamed Smasher.

No one listened. Smasher's lousy world had just got even more lousy.

Later that week, something happened.

It was on a night that followed a day that had been pretty much like every day before that. A day when Smasher had been thrown off the bus for spraying graffiti. A day when he'd nicked two kids' phones, spat at a teacher, and had his new army knife confiscated for cutting up his maths book. Because man, maths was sooooooo boring!

That night, as Smasher tried to sleep, a strange figure appeared at the end of his bed. Was he dreaming, or was it for real?

Whatever, Smasher felt scared. If only he had a hammer or a gun or something, he could smash its stupid brains out.

The figure spoke, 'My name is Gor.' His voice boomed across the room.

'What terrible things have happened to you Smasher, to make you so full of fire? Sometimes you seem more like a bomb than a boy.'

Gor continued, 'Smasher, you've taken the wrong turning.'
'What do you mean?' Smasher snapped, really angry now.
'You've taken the turning to Smash-it-Up. You've missed the
turning called Special.'

'Go to hell, you crazy weirdo! Get out of my room!'
screamed Smasher.

Gor carried on speaking, 'We'll need to visit both places,'
he said.

Before he knew it, Smasher was being sucked into an icy tunnel.

He was travelling so fast, he couldn't breathe properly, turning upside down, round and round like a hundred mile-an-hour, death-dealing spinning-top.
Then **thump**!

'We're here', said Gor. 'We've arrived at Smash-it-Up.'

When Smasher looked around, he saw a deep dark space. The air was heavy and rotten. Piercing sounds hurt his ears.

When he looked closer, he saw people burning on stakes. Crowds were cheering as heads were chopped off.

Some people were dragged along in chains and whipped, to make them walk faster.

Where am I? It's so dark and rotten here. Everyone is being hurt or killed.

Others were thrown into dungeons and told they would stay there forever.

Then Smasher saw whole cities blown up, and people losing their homes, running for their lives. They didn't make it.

He saw flames tearing through buildings and soldiers falling in front of guns firing at them. They all died.

Then an almighty explosion brought black rains from the skies. There was screaming and terror everywhere. Bodies in piles all over the ground. The air was thick with hate.

'Is this hell?' asked Smasher.
'No', said Gor, 'It's earth.'

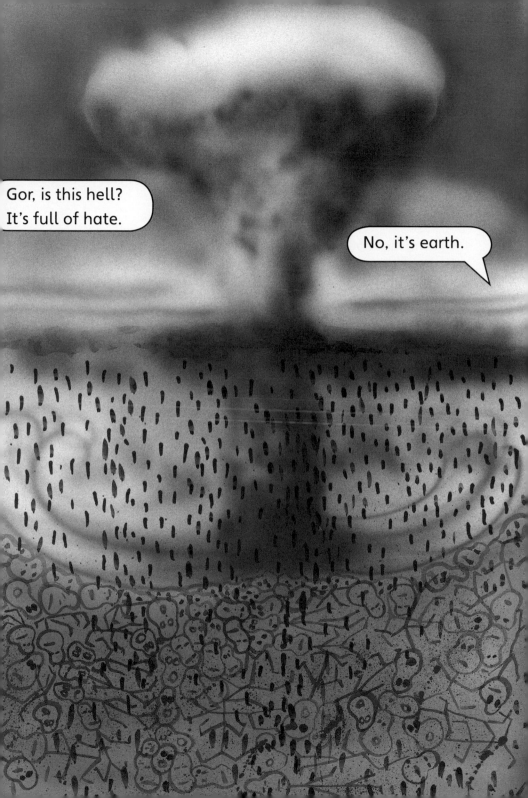

As Smasher sat with all the screaming and the dead, Gor continued, 'See how easy it is to smash and kill?' he said. 'Anyone can do it.' In fact smashing is so ordinary that people have been doing it for thousands of years.'

'But how did it get to be like this?' asked Smasher, stunned by what he was seeing.

'Many reasons', said Gor, 'But often it starts when adults see only bad things, not good, in kids. When they really hurt them and don't see their loneliness and pain. Then those kids, burned by life, scream their rage into the world.'

Smasher looked far into the distance, in silence.

'But now it's time to visit Special', said Gor.

Before Smasher could protest, he was whisked off his feet just like before. But this time, he was lifted by a warm breeze. It felt like riding on a soft cushion rather than hurtling down that awful tunnel.

Then **thump**!

Smasher looked around. They had landed in a field by a river.

The first thing Smasher heard was laughter.

And everywhere he looked, people were having fun. A group of boys were making model boats. Someone was arranging a surprise for a friend's birthday. A woman moved a baby bird out of the road and put it back with its mother.

When Smasher blinked and looked again, he saw people inventing cars and computers and planes that could travel faster than the speed of sound. He saw doctors inventing medicines to help thousands of people live instead of die. He saw important looking people sitting around a table, talking about how to stop people fighting each other and the planet from coming to any more harm.

But most amazing of all there was Grant, looking straight at Smasher, smiling.

Smasher felt that this was the coolest place.

Suddenly in the midst of it all, there was his climbing wall. Smasher was so excited to see it. But then there was a terrible scream. A little boy had fallen off the wall.

Smasher rushed over, picked him up, and held him in his arms. But the child's crying went on and on, as if forever. 'Has this one been burned by life?' asked Smasher.

'I think you know that', Gor replied.

Smasher's shirt was wet with the boy's tears but something
made him want to stay just holding him.
Then Gor's voice echoed all around.
'How will **you** use this life Smasher?' he said.
'How will you walk this planet?
You have learned to play this life for pain.
You think you're winning, but you're losing.'

Smasher was both hearing the words, and yet he wasn't,
because something had happened. He had looked right into
the little boy's eyes. Then he knew …

The child was a younger Smasher. The time when his father
had walked out and his mother drank all the time. He
remembered how awful it had felt. Like he was falling off the
highest wall in the whole world, like he was drowning in a
great pit of screaming, with no one to turn to.

Mum drunk.
Dad gone.

Suddenly, everything went dark.
The dream, or whatever it had been, was over.

A week later, Smasher had the best day of his life. Grant had arranged to take the climbing club into the country. They met really early outside Grant's house, just by the Old Bull pub. They got into the minibus and sang all the way there.

They climbed one rock face after another, each one steeper than the last, with more and more difficult moves.

It was so cool.

Smasher always seemed to be able to work out how to shift his weight, and move his hands and feet to get a steady position.

Afterwards they all sat by the river eating sandwiches. 'Hey Asher you did just great', said Grant, and Smasher felt great.

On the way back, the minibus dropped them back at the Old Bull. Smasher caught the bus home. He was feeling on top of the world.

Then on the bus he saw two of his best mates, Bentley and Tyson who lived down his street. Smasher knew from Bentley's face that something was wrong.

'Glad you're here Smasher', said Bentley. 'Things are getting ugly. That kid you beat up at school, Smithie, well his big bro' came looking for you. When he couldn't find you, him and his gang went to your place and smashed up your bike.'

As he thought of his bike in bits, Smasher felt his blood boil. Pain seared through his heart. It would have to be WAR. Nothing else would do.

They went for a drink at the burger bar. They plotted and plotted.

They were going to pay back Smithie's brother, once and for all.

That night, just as Smasher was falling asleep, Gor appeared again.

'Smasher, you're standing at the crossroads', he said. 'The crossroads that lead either to Special or Smash-it-Up. You've got a choice. You could spend the rest of your life in either.'

Smasher told him to shut up and get out of his life.

But Gor didn't stop there. 'I want something better for you in this life. I want you to dream great things. But for that you'll need one thing.'

Smasher's curiosity got the better of him. 'What's that?' he asked, in spite of himself.

'Someone who believes in you. Someone who doesn't see you as scum.' Gor paused, and then continued, 'The problem is that smashers are often so angry, they walk straight past the people who believe in them. They don't trust them, even smash up their kindness...'

And with that, Gor was gone.

In the morning, Smasher's alarm clock woke him up. He felt awful.

The next night Bentley, Tyson and Smasher set off for revenge.
They'd planned some really neat pay back. They were going
to find Smithie's brother's car, slash the tyres, smash the
windows, burn cigarettes into the seats, spray it with red paint
and maybe even torch it.

The buzz, the POWER surging through Smasher's veins.
Nothing like it! The thought of making that scumbag squirm,
giving him a taste of his own medicine. After all, it was only
justice!

What was that thing someone said in the Bible about
revenge? 'An eye for an eye and a tooth for a tooth!'

The three of them went off, armed with spray paint, hammers and matches, high on excitement and adventure. Bentley had brought beer and a spliff to get rid of the fear.

As they turned down past the old pub and on to the crossroads, Bentley asked, 'Which way now, Smasher?'

But then something happened. Smasher looked at the signpost. He just couldn't take his eyes off it.

Instead of saying 'Beddington Road' and 'George Street', which it had always done, it read 'Special' and 'Smash-it-Up'.

And to make matters worse, Gor's words started ringing in his ears: 'You've got a choice.'

Smasher felt very hot, like he was going to faint. Thoughts flooded through his mind. Torch the car? That's serious. Were they going too far this time? What if he got caught and sent to jail?

'Which way, cloth ears, which way is it?' Bentley was asking him again.

Smasher's heart was pounding and pounding. His hands were clammy with sweat.He dropped everything he was carrying and ran.

He ran and ran, back through the street, over the wall, down to the flats by the school, until he arrived back at the pub.

He knocked on Grant's door.

The door opened. 'HELP!', said Smasher. 'Help me Grant, help me.'

He didn't know what he was saying, but the words kept coming out. 'You've got to help me. I was the little boy who fell off the wall. You've got to know. It was me. It was ME.'

There was a loud siren. Tyres screeching to a halt. Cars were pulling up...

....it was the police.

Simon Asher, now twenty, was on a climb in the country, when his phone rang. It was Grant.

'Hi Asher. Look we've got these kids. The school, they're worried about them, can you help?'

'Sure', said Asher, 'I'll come over to the gym tonight.'

SIX YEARS LATER ...
Hi, Grant. Some kids in trouble at school? Yeah, I'll come and help. See you later.

When he got there, some rough looking kids were hanging about. They'd been sent there by the Headteacher for causing trouble in the school, stealing, breaking windows, fighting, the usual things.

If you'd been there that evening you'd have seen Asher take out a large piece of paper. You'd have seen him draw a crossroads, and a big signpost and write in big letters:

SOMEONE WHO BELIEVES IN YOU.

You'd have heard him talk to the kids about his own life. You'd have heard his voice get louder and firmer when he said, 'I want more for you than this lousy world.'

You'd have seen two of the boys mock him, murmuring 'Crazy weirdo', while others fidgeted uncomfortably. They all knew about Asher. They knew he was a champion climbing instructor, who'd won lots of trophies and that he was one of the coolest guys in town.

Some of the kids walked off swearing and shouting. 'You on something Asher?' 'Waste of space.'

But a few of the others stayed.

Ten months later Grant met Asher on the street.

'You did great with those kids Asher. Three of them went back to school, asked for help. They're doing really well on the job scheme now, Engineering, ICT, all sorts of things.'

'And the rest?' asked Asher.

'They were thrown out of school, in trouble with the police for usual things – knives, drugs.'

Asher felt awful. If only he'd found better words, been clearer, listened to them more. Perhaps then he could have saved them from taking the wrong turning.

Asher turned to Grant. 'I didn't do enough.'

Grant looked at him. 'You did so much. You DO so much.'

That night, there was Gor in his room again, just as he had been six years ago. Asher wondered why. After all, he didn't need him now.

The world was no longer a lousy place for him, but a special place he cared about a lot.

But he did have a question for Gor. He had remembered something in that book his teacher had read to the class, 'Human beings will not rest until they have destroyed everything beautiful in the world.'

So with a certain desperation in his voice, Asher asked Gor the most important question of all…

'What will we do in the end?'

'Will so many people go to Smash-it-Up, that one day we smash up the whole wide world?'

'Or will Special become stronger, so there's a kinder world, just in time, before it's too late?'

'We don't know', said Gor. 'We just don't know.'

About the Authors

Dr **Margot Sunderland** is Director of Education and Training at The Centre for Child Mental Health and Honorary Visiting Fellow, London Metropolitan University. She is a child psychotherapist with more than 20 years' experience of working with children and young people. She is also a Founding Director of the British Accredited Higher Education College, The Institute for Arts in Therapy and Education which runs MA Emotional Literacy for Children and MA Integrative Child Psychotherapy.

Nicky Armstrong holds an MA from the Slade School of Fine Art and a BA Hons in Theatre Design from the University of Central England. For many years she was a tutor in *trompe l'œil* at The Hampstead School of Decorative Arts, London. She is the principal artist at The London Art House. She has illustrated over 20 books, which have been published in many countries. Nicky has also achieved major commissions nationally and internationally in mural work and fine art.